The Brothers Jacob (1785-1863) And Willhelm (1786-1859) Grimm

This book contains one of the hundreds of wonderful fairy tales collected by the Brothers Grimm.

Many of these stories, such as Cinderella, Snow White, Hansel and Gretel, The Prince and the Frog, Tom Thumb, and others, are so well known that it seems as though we were born with them. Many other beautiful and fantastical tales are lesser known and should be made available to a wider readership.

Jacob Grimm was born in 1785 and his brother Willhelm a year later. The brothers were also writers and carried out research into the German language and folklore but became world famous for the fairy tales they collected and published over the years. These were tales which had been passed down from generation to generation without ever being written down.

The stories were collected from many people over a period of many years but their main and richest source was a woman cow-herd called Katerina Weimann. She knew by heart literally hundreds of traditional tales which the Brothers Grimm faithfully recorded. The Brothers Grimm worked for sixteen years before publishing the first volume of these tales, and three years later, in 1815, their second book was published. These tales, originally published in German, have been translated over the years into scores of other languages and have given endless pleasure to many generations of children all over the globe.

Adapted by: Yossi Bechar & David Kriss
Illustrations: Tuvia Kurtz

Book Design: Arie Bodian
Assistant Editor: Yossi Ladislav Silber
Graphic Layout: Orly Golan

ISBN 965-312-016-6
Produced by I.C.F. Inc. P.O.Box 1528 Radio City Station N.Y.C., N.Y. 10101
Kidfest International is a registered trade mark of
International Children's Festival Inc.
Cat. No. B-43003

Little Red Riding Hood

by the Brothers Grimm

Kidfest
INTERNATIONAL

In fairy tales the very first line
Is always "Once upon a time,"
And let me whisper in your ear
Something else I'd like you to hear:
When you're reading fairy tales
Don't worry about all the details.
It doesn't matter if they're true
As long as they are true for you.
Well, that's all I wanted to say
So let's read the story without further delay...

Little Red Riding Hood

nce upon a time, at the wood's edge,
Lived a happy family in a little cottage.
There was a mother, a father and a sweet little girl-
A beautiful child with golden curls.

At the other edge of the wood lived grandmother,
And they would often go to visit each other
For grandmother loved her pretty grandaughter
Just as all grandmothers oughter.
And the grandaughter loved her grandmother too
Just as all grandaughters ought to do.
She would run into her arms when they came to her home
And grandmother would say, "Oooh, look how you've grown!"

As a birthday present for her little grandaughter
Grandmother went out and bought her
A wonderful gift - a new red dress
With a little white apron, and what was best -
A beautiful, fine-spun silk red hood.
The little grandaughter did look good.
Every single place she went
People paied her compliments.
In fact her hood was such a hit
She got a name because of it.
"Little Red Riding Hood!" the people proclaimed
And so "Little Red Riding Hood" became her nickname.
Little Red Riding Hood with her golden curls
Was a very, very good little girl.
She did whatever her mother said,
She loved to tidy her room and make her own bed,
But she loved one thing more than any other,
And that was to visit her grandmother.

One day, grandmother fell ill.
Mother explained that she had caught a chill
And the doctor had told her stay in bed.
"Oh poor grandmother!" Red Riding Hood said.
"She must feel so sad there all alone.
I wish I could go and cheer her up at home."
"You're right," said mother,
"And it's a very kind thought,
But still, I really think we ought
To wait a few days until grandmother feels well."
"But she's lonely!" cried Red Riding Hood,
"I know, I can tell!

And a few days is a long time when you're ill
And you're lying in bed, and you've got to stay still."

Mother looked down at her daughter with pride,
She thought for a while and then she sighed,
"All right then daughter, you can have your own way.
In fact you can even go today.
I'll fill a basket with something to eat,
And you can take it to grandmother as a treat."
In a basket mother put cheese and bread,
"Grandmother will be happy to get this," she said.
Then she added some cookies and a jar of broth
And covered the basket with a cloth.
"That's all," said mother,
"Now you should be on your way.
You'd better hurry while it's still day.

The wood is no place to be at night.
A little girl like you could get a fright.
Now remember to stay on the path all the time.
You know where it is, just follow the signs.
And don't talk to strangers
Whatever they say.
You don't know who they are
And they might lead you astray."
Little Red Riding Hood nodded her head.
She understood everything mother had said.
"Don't worry mother, I'll take care.
I won't stop even once until I get there."
Mother gave her a kiss and told her to be good
And Little Red Riding Hood set off into the wood.
Her new red suit stood out sharply against the green
And this meant that she could easily be seen.

It was a beautiful day!
Fresh mushrooms glittered white beneath the trees,
Multicolored birds twittered happily,
Little baby deer peeked shyly through the leaves,
And Red Riding Hood would soon be at grandmother's,
Or so she believed...

Now deep in the wood, between the trees,
Lurked a hungry wolf, who licked his lips with glee.
He had spotted Red Riding Hood walking down the path
And as soon as he saw her he began to laugh,
"Ho! That basket must be full of tasty stuff.
I'll be able to snatch that easily enough.
And that little girl would be wonderful to chew
But to eat her I'll need to use a trick or two."
The wolf leaped out and stood in her way
But Little Red Riding Hood wasn't afraid.
She didn't know that hungry wolves attack
And that to the wolf, she looked like a tasty snack.
The wolf said,
"Hello little girl, what is your name?
And why are you walking alone down the lane?"
Red Riding Hood said,
"My name is Red Riding Hood
And I am walking through the wood
To visit my grandmother who is sick."
The wolf gave his lips another lick.
This was too good to be true.
He'd eat the girl and the grandmother too!
All he had to do was think up some delay,
To keep the girl in the woods,
And then he'd run away
To eat grandmother for his tea.
Oh how tasty she would be!
And when Red Riding Hood arrived
He'd gobble her up in no time.
The wolf's eyes took on an ugly leer.
What a wonderful idea!

The wolf said,
"If you want to make your grandmother well,
I've got an idea that's really swell.
Why not pick some flowers along the way?
They'll make her room look so happy and gay.
There's nothing as cheering as a bouquet of flowers.
She'll be able to look at them for hours and hours!"
"Oh yes!" cried Little Red Riding Hood.
"I can see, Mr. Wolf, that your heart is good.
I think that that's a beautiful idea.
Oh look, there are some flowers over here!
Grandmother will get a lovely surprise."
And she began to pick flowers of every color and size.

Meanwhile, the wolf ran as fast as he could
To grandmother's house at the edge of the wood.
He raced all the way without even stopping
And burst into the house without even knocking.
Nobody heard and nobody saw
As he attacked poor grandmother with terrible roar.
She didn't stand a chance of course
And was swallowed whole in his ugly jaws.

"Mmmmm," grinned the wolf, "that tasted good.
Now I've got to get ready to trap Red Riding Hood."
He put on grandmother's white nightdress,
Pulled the blankets up over his chest,
On his head he put grandmother's sleeping cap
And then lay back in bed as though taking a nap.

"Aha!" he thought in his cruel mind,
"Red Riding Hood will taste divine!"

Meanwhile, back in the wood,
There was Little Red Riding Hood
With a bunch of flowers in her hand.
"Oh my!" she cried, "they do look grand.
It's the very best present I could find.
That nice old wolf was certainly kind.
And now I'd better be on my way
While I can still see by the light of day."
To grandmother's house Red Riding Hood hurried.
She felt very happy and not at all worried.
For soon, she believed, she would see her grandmother
And they always had such a good time with each other.
Red Riding Hood of course had no way of knowing
What had happened to grandmother
And that she was not going
To see her lying there in bed
But to meet the wolf lying there instead!

Red Riding Hood reached the door and walked through.
She called out, "Grandmother! Hello! How are you?
Look, I've brought lots of things to eat
And this bunch of flowers. Aren't they sweet?"
Silence... there was no reply,
So Red Riding Hood gave another try.
"Grandmother! Grandmother?
It's me, Red Riding Hood!"
Then a strange voice answered,
"Oh, it's you grandaughter... good.
I'm so glad you came to visit today.
Come into the bedroom dear, right this way.
I'm too weak to get out of bed I'm afraid."

Red Riding Hood walked into grandmother's bedroom.
It was dark and hard to see in the gloom.
She couldn't make out who was lying in the bed
But thought it must be grandmother
For there was a nightcap on her head.
Red Riding Hood said,
"It's so dark in here grandmother
I'll let in some light."
"No, no no..." croaked the wolf,
"It's quite all right.
The shutters are closed on the doctor's advice
Because too much light hurts my eyes."
Little Red Riding Hood still had no idea
That the wolf was in the bed
But when she drew near
And offered the wolf some of the food,
He wolfed it down in a way that was so rude,
And made so many grunting sounds
That it gave her a fright.
Something about grandmother wasn't quite right.
Red Riding Hood moved closer so she could see
And studied grandmother carefully.
There seemed to be something wrong with her ears.
They were unusually small, but now they appeared
To be big and grey and covered with hair.
In fact they looked like a very strange pair.
She stared at her grandmother's ears then at last
She decided some questions ought to be asked.
"Grandmother, why are your ears so very big?"
"Why are my ears so very big?
All the better to hear you with!"

Said the crafty wolf with an evil leer.
Little Red Riding Hood brought her face near.
Under her reading glasses, grandmother's eyes
Where quite red, and twice their regular size.
"Grandmother, why are your eyes so big?"
"What's that?" said the wolf,
"Why my eyes are so big?
All the better to see you with!"
Then Red Riding Hood saw something beyond belief.

She looked into her grandmother's mouth
And saw the size of her teeth.
And when she saw the shape of her fangs
Her little heart began to bang.
"Grandmother... why are your teeth s..so big??"
"All the better to eat you with!
Now I've got you in my trap!"
Snarled the evil wolf and his big jaws snapped.
He threw the glasses off his nose.

Poor Little Red Riding Hood just froze.
Instead of her dear old sick grandmother
A growling wolf leaped from under the covers.
Little Red Riding Hood began to scream,
"Help! Help! Save me! Please!"
But the wolf seemed completely at his ease.
"You little fool," he smiled, "go ahead and shout.
The wood is empty, there's no-one about."

But the wolf was the fool and not Red Riding Hood
For who should be passing through the wood
But a brave hunter who heard her shouts
And turned and ran straight into the house.
He saw that the wolf was about to kill her,
He raised his gun and pressed the trigger...
And before the wolf could close his fangs,
The gun went off with a mighty bang.

The wicked wolf clutched at the bed,
Closed his eyes, and fell down dead.
Poor Red Riding Hood had got a terrible fright,
But the hunter said,
"There, there, it's all right.
The wolf is dead, that's for sure.
He won't be bothering you any more.
"Thank you dear hunter," cried Red Riding Hood
"You saved me!
I'd be eaten up if it wasn't for your bravery.
Can you help me find my grandmother too?
She's disappeared and I don't know what to do."
They searched in all the rooms,
They looked through the yard,
They even looked under the bed,
Then the hunter stared hard
At the evil wolf lying dead on the floor
And said, "I've got something to tell you
You should prepare yourself for.
I think your grandmother's been eaten up
And is lying right now in the wolf's stomach!"

Little Red Riding Hood cried and cried,
But the hunter said,
"Don't you worry, dry your eyes.
It didn't happen long ago
And I'm sure she's still alive.

The hunter took out his hunting knife,
Slit the wolf's stomach open
And grandmother was alive!

It was as though the wolf had never attacked.
"Oh dear grandmother", cried Red Riding Hood,
"We've got you back!"

Grandmother hugged her little grandaughter
And kissed the brave hunter who had fought for her,
"Thank you good hunter, you're a brave man and true.
Where would we be if it wasn't for you!"
Then they all sat down thankfully
And with Red Riding Hood's food
Had a wonderful tea.

Now I'm sure that you'll ask your father or mother
Questions like, "How come grandmother
Was still alive when she was pulled out?"
And other questions which fill you with doubt.
Well, that's what I meant at the start of this tale
When I said not to worry about the details.
It doesn't matter if it's true
As long as it's true for you.
And so...

Grandmother and Little Red Riding Hood
Lived happily ever after in the wood.

From the Classic Fairy Tales Series

Cat. No.   Title